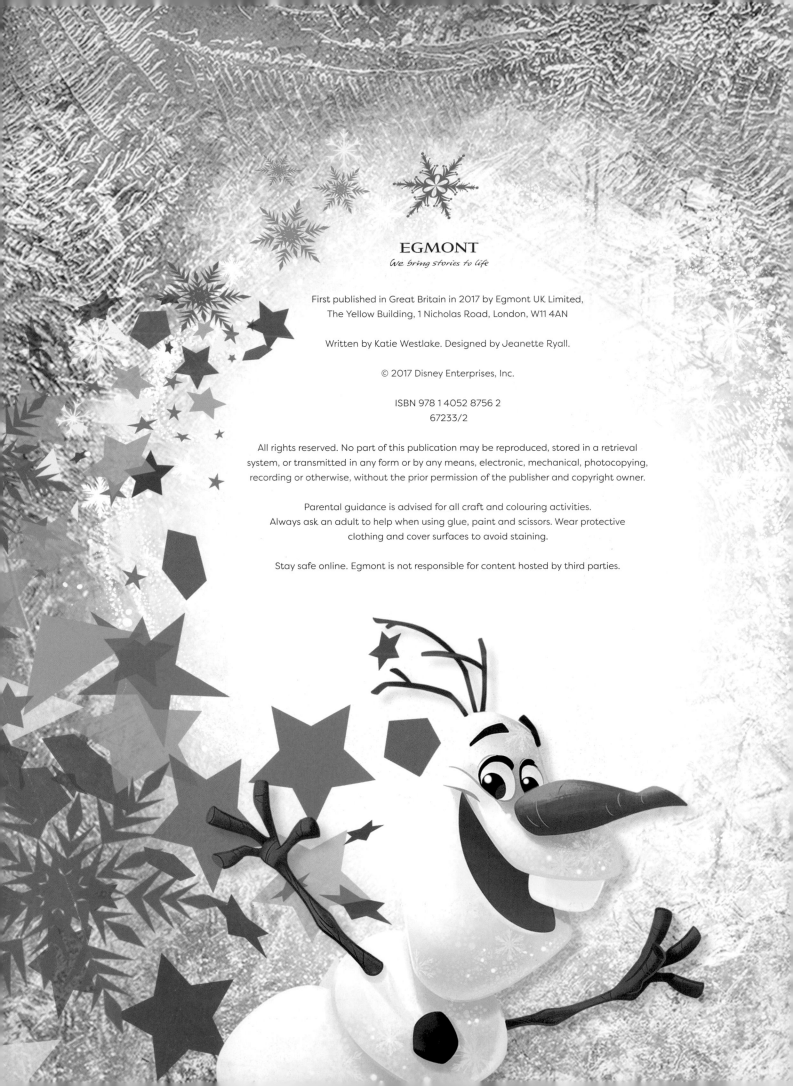

EGMONT

We bring stories to life

First published in Great Britain in 2017 by Egmont UK Limited,
The Yellow Building, 1 Nicholas Road, London, W11 4AN

Written by Katie Westlake. Designed by Jeanette Ryall.

© 2017 Disney Enterprises, Inc.

ISBN 978 1 4052 8756 2
67233/2

Parental guidance is advised for all craft and colouring activities.
Always ask an adult to help when using glue, paint and scissors. Wear protective clothing and cover surfaces to avoid staining.

Stay safe online. Egmont is not responsible for content hosted by third parties.

From the Movie

Disney
FROZEN

ANNUAL
2018

This Frozen Annual belongs to:

....
Write your name here.

From the Movie

CONTENTS

All About Elsa

Add some icy colour to this picture of Elsa.

Elsa is the first-born royal sister, and the Queen of Arendelle. Using her magical powers, she is able to control ice and snow. Elsa spent most of her life trying to hide her magic, but this led to disaster, Arendelle was plunged into an eternal winter! With her sister Anna's help, she learned the key to controlling her powers, and brought summer back to Arendelle.

Elsa's Winter Words

Elsa is thinking about her favourite winter words.
Trace over the letters to find out what they are.

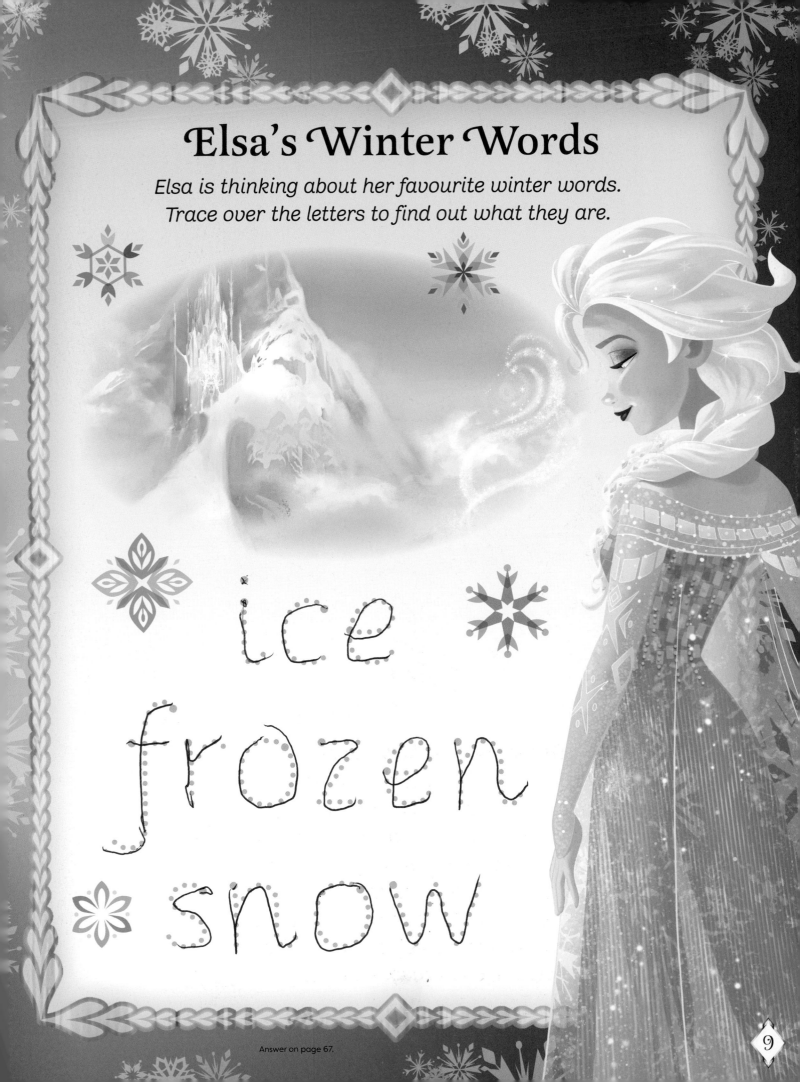

ice

frozen

snow

THE KINGDOM OF ARENDELLE

Arendelle is home to Anna, Elsa and all their friends.
Solve these puzzles to find out some of the places they visit.

Write the missing letters in the spaces.

1

_ORTH

MOU_TAI_

2

TRO_ _

VA_ _EY

3

AR_ND_ LL_

Unscramble the letters to reveal the place names.

5 TASCEL

4 EIC CALAPE

6 DJOFR

11

WINTER MAGIC

Elsa is making spectacular ice ornaments for the castle.
Draw lines to complete the grid so that each row
and column contains one of each sculpture.

Surprise!

Join the dots to draw
this holiday classic!

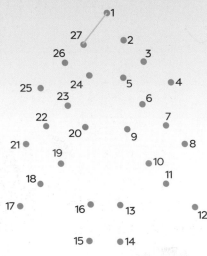

Answers on page 67.

PALACE MEMORIES

Elsa uses her magic to make the snowgies, Olaf and even an Ice Palace!
Look at the picture below, then hide it with a piece of paper.
Now try to answer the quiz questions below.

1

Who is Sven
standing next to?

2

What is Olaf
looking at?

3

How many characters
in the picture aren't
made from snow?

4

Are Elsa and Anna
in the picture?

Answers on page 67.

A LOYAL GUARD

Elsa created Marshmallow to guard the Ice Palace. Although at first he may seem a little frosty, he is a really loyal protector. Can you spot which picture below is the odd one out?

a
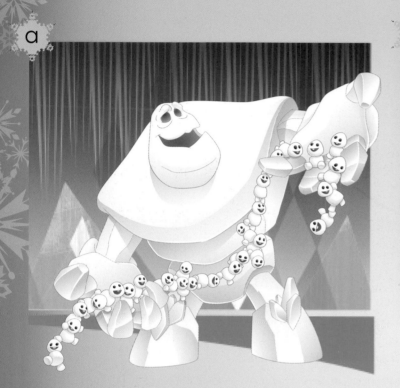

b

c
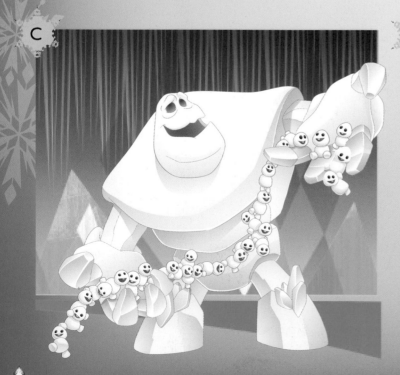

d
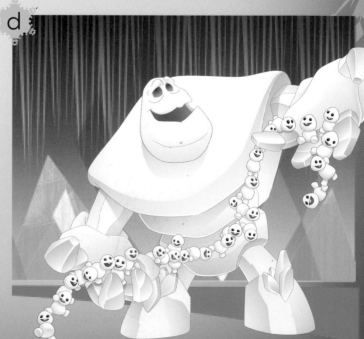

Answer on page 67.

HAPPY MOMENTS

It's so fun to open presents together! Number the jumbled sections from 1 to 7 to match the happy scene below.

Tick the boxes as you find the 6 blue gifts in the top scene.

ALL ABOUT ANNA

Colour in this pretty picture of Anna.

Anna is Elsa's younger sister. She used to feel alone in the castle, and didn't understand why Elsa didn't want to play with her anymore. When she discovered Elsa's powers, she never gave up on her sister, and showed her the way to save the kingdom. From then on, life in Arendelle was very different. Anna is adventurous, chatty and a little clumsy!

Lost in the Snow

Anna is looking for Kristoff in the snow. Help her find him by guiding her through the maze.

START ▶

◀ FINISH

FROZEN GAME

Can you help Anna and Elsa end the eternal winter?
Find a friend, a dice and two counters. Take turns
to throw the dice and see who finishes first!

START

1

2

12 — A friendly snowman agrees to help you. Move on two spaces.

13

14

15 — A scary snowman chases you away. Move back one space.

17 — You receive helpful advice from the trolls. Move on one space.

16

18

4

An ice harvester gives you a lift on his sleigh. Move on one space.

5

6

A pack of hungry wolves chases you. Move back one space.

3

7

8

You pass Oaken's shop and collect a warm coat. Move on one space.

9

10

You fall into a snowdrift. Move back one space.

11

19

Prince Hans locks you in the castle. Move back one space.

20

Well done! You brought summer back to Arendelle!

FINISH

A Special Snowman

Anna and Elsa are building a snowman! Follow the snowflake trail and complete the activities to find out who this happy snowman is.

1

What do you need to make a snowman? Fill in the missing letters.

S _ _ W

2

Pick the perfect carrot by finding the odd one out.

a
b
c
d

4

Copy the letters into their matching coloured boxes to find out his name.

A F O L

3

How many pieces of coal does this snowman have?

Colour in Olaf.

5

You've built a merry little snowman. Trace over the dotted line to draw him yourself.

Is it Time Yet?

IT'S A NICE WINTER DAY ...

WHEN ARE WE GOING OUT WITH KRISTOFF AND SVEN? I CAN'T WAIT!

LATER, OLAF! IT'S ONLY 1 O'CLOCK AND WE'RE MEETING THEM AT 3 O'CLOCK!

WHEN THE SHORT HAND IS ON 3, WE'LL GO OUT!

?

HMMM ... REALLY?!?

THAT'S EASY, ALL YOU HAVE TO DO IS ...

WHAT ARE YOU DOING?

POING!

LOOK! IT'S TIME TO GO!

HA, HA, THAT'S VERY SMART, OLAF!

Manuscript: Tea Orsi; Layout: Emilio Urbano; Cleanup: Nicoletta Baldari; Colour: Dario Calabria

The End

PUZZLING PATHS

Olaf can't wait to meet up with Anna, Kristoff and Sven, but where are his friends? Follow the paths to see which one leads to each friend.

Anna

Kristoff

Sven

a

b

c

Answers on page 67

ALL ABOUT OLAF

Add some colour to Olaf.

Olaf is a happy little snowman who loves warm hugs! Elsa created him with her magical powers and named him herself. Olaf agrees to help Anna save Arendelle, as he longs to see the summer sun. Olaf is very loyal and would melt for any of his friends.

Fun in the Sun

Olaf loves everything about summer!
Can you find the summery words in this word search?

Sun

Hot

Flowers

Bees

Tanned

Relax

t	a	b	e	e	s	e	m	o
k	l	c	r	y	u	t	a	l
t	x	y	a	f	n	r	a	w
a	s	u	x	h	a	q	l	e
n	t	f	l	o	w	e	r	s
n	e	c	t	t	a	n	b	t
e	n	o	w	f	l	a	s	e
d	u	l	r	e	e	s	u	r
i	y	d	t	r	e	l	a	x

A Day at the Beach

Manuscript: Tea Orsi; Layout: Alberto Zanon; Cleanup: Veronica Di Lorenzo; Colour: Manuela Nerolini

SUMMER TRIP

Elsa, Anna and Olaf are going on a summer trip!
Tick the details below when you spot them in the picture.

Let's Go

Follow the blue arrows and guide the friends along the flowery path.

Trace the letters to find out where the friends are going.

To the

woods

PRETTY BUTTERFLIES

You will need:

2 coloured paper squares (15 x 15cm)

Pipe cleaner cut to 15cm

Optional: Thin ribbon or
yarn to hang

 1 Fold the paper in half diagonally to make a triangle.

 **2** Working from the centre line out, make zig zag folds about 1cm apart, to one half, then the other. Repeat with the second piece of paper.

 3 Pinch together at the centre. Wrap firmly with the pipe cleaner and twist to secure. Bend the ends of the pipe cleaner to make antennae.

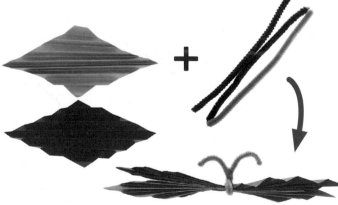

4 Open up the wings and flatten the edges to create the wing shape. You could hang your butterfly up with ribbon or yarn.

WARM HUGS

Olaf can't choose who to hug next! Help him decide by working out who comes next in each sequence.

Answer on page 67.

Disney
FROZEN FEVER

It was Anna's birthday and Elsa was determined to make it the best birthday ever. After shutting Anna out for all those years, Elsa wanted her to have the perfect day. Kristoff, Elsa, Olaf and Sven were in the courtyard. Elsa was decorating the cake, but she couldn't decide what should go on the top.

"Come on Elsa, this is for Anna. You can do this!" Elsa whispered, as she created a beautiful ice sculpture with her magic. "I just want everything to be perfect." "Speaking of perfect ... check this out!" Kristoff said. He stood back to admire his creation. A great big banner stretched across the courtyard. It said 'Happy Birthday Anna' in colourful letters.

Elsa, Kristoff and Sven looked around the courtyard.

"Olaf, what are you doing?" Elsa cried.

Olaf was stuffing handfuls of cake into his mouth. He looked at the ground sheepishly.

"Sorry Elsa," Olaf mumbled through the cake in his mouth. It was time to wake Anna and start the celebrations. Elsa left Kristoff in charge of the courtyard.

"Don't touch anything!" she called, as she went into the castle.

When she reached Anna's room, Elsa gently shook Anna awake saying, "Wake up Anna, it's your birthday!"

33

Slowly Anna got out of bed, and Elsa hurried her over to the dressing room. She handed over Anna's first present, a brand new outfit. Whilst Anna dressed, Elsa explained that she was going to make this the most perfect day ever. As she said this she sneezed loudly, and two little snowmen popped into the air!

The sisters didn't notice them scurrying towards the courtyard. "Elsa, I think you have a cold," Anna said. Elsa shook her head, "A cold never bothered me anyway."

In a flurry of magic, Elsa changed into a party dress and flowers sparkled all over Anna's dress and in her hair. She showed Anna the end of a piece of string, that led out of the bedroom and into the corridor. "Just follow the string!" Elsa said. Anna followed the string through the castle where Elsa had hidden lots of presents. A clock, a bracelet, a portrait and even a sandwich. Anna was delighted with every one!

They made their way out of the castle where Elsa had even more birthday surprises in store.

Elsa led a choir of children in a birthday song for Anna, and they stopped by Oaken's Cloakens to pick up a new cloak.

As they collected more of Anna's presents, Elsa's sneezing was getting worse. Each time she sneezed, lots of new little snowmen popped into the air. Anna tried to make Elsa rest in bed, but she refused.

In the courtyard, Kristoff, Olaf and Sven were trying to control every little snowman Elsa had created with her sneezing. The snowmen knocked over the punch bowl, ripped down the sign and tried to eat the birthday cake!

Olaf did his best to fix the birthday banner, but he couldn't read or spell! Kristoff looked at the sign in despair.

35

Meanwhile, Elsa and Anna climbed the clock tower, but Elsa was getting weaker with every step. When they reached the top, Elsa nearly fell from the tower. Luckily Anna pulled her back just in time.

"Elsa you need to rest," Anna insisted. "You have a fever!"

As they made their way back to the castle, Elsa said she was sorry for ruining Anna's birthday. Anna told her that she hadn't ruined anything, but that she was worried about Elsa and that she should go to bed.

They walked through the gates and everyone in the courtyard yelled "SURPRISE!" Kristoff, Olaf and Sven had managed to fix the sign and stop the snowmen from eating the cake.

Anna was amazed. Olaf and the children of Arendelle lifted Anna onto their shoulders, and the little snowmen spelled out 'ANNA' in the sky. Kristoff presented the cake and Sven cut it with his antlers, so everyone could have a piece.

A little while later, Anna helped Elsa into bed. "That was the best birthday present ever," whispered Anna. "Which one?" Elsa asked. "You letting me take care of you," Anna replied.

The End

ALL ABOUT KRISTOFF

Add some colours to Kristoff.

Kristoff was raised in the mountains by the trolls. His best buddy is Sven, a reindeer, who pulls his sleigh. Kristoff is an ice harvester, and agrees to help Anna climb the North Mountain in return for supplies. Despite his tough exterior, Kristoff is desperate to save Anna and help her find her sister.

Kristoff's Title

Anna has given Kristoff an Official title! Colour in every 'X' and write the remaining letters in the space below to find out what it is.

X	I	X	X	X	C	X	X
E	X	M	X	X	X	A	X
X	S	X	T	X	X	X	E
X	X	X	X	R	X	X	X

Arendelle's
Official

_ _ _

_ _ _ _ _ _

And Deliverer

SPECIAL DELIVERY

Kristoff is bringing presents for Anna and Elsa – they're going to celebrate together! Enter the tree maze and help him find the right path to Arendelle castle!

FINISH

START

40

What is Kristoff saying to Sven? Follow the paths and write the letters in the spaces to find out.

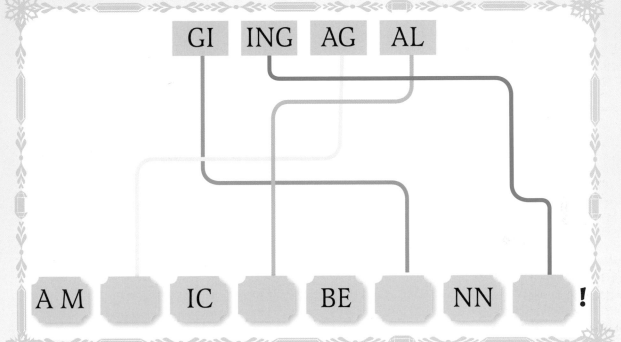

GI ING AG AL

A M ___ IC ___ BE ___ NN ___ !

Present fun

Add some great colour to the presents.

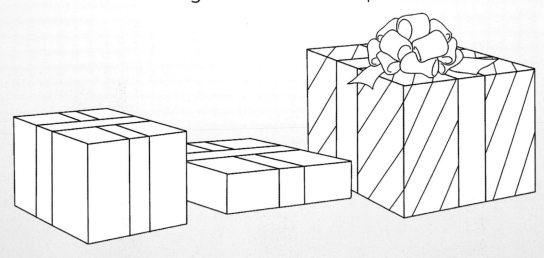

SNOW BUDDIES

How well do you know these two best friends? Read the questions below, then circle the correct picture to answer each question.

1

Whose favourite snack is a carrot?

2

Who sang, "Reindeers are better than people ..."?

3

Who first met Anna in Oaken's Shop?

4

Who do Sven and Kristoff agree smells better?

5

Who is a bit of a fixer-upper?

Answer on page 68.

A FIXER UPPER

Part of Kristoff is missing from the picture below. Can you fix him by joining up the numbered dots? Then colour the picture.

WHERE IS EVERYONE?

Manuscript: Tea Orsi; Layout: Zanon Alberto; Cleanup: Veronica Di Lorenzo; Colour: Dario Calabria

The End

FUNNY SNOWGIES

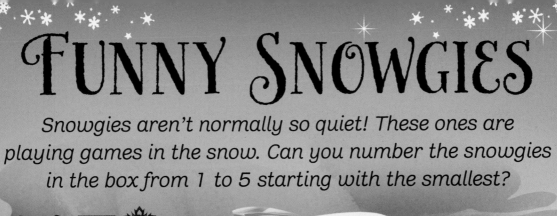

Snowgies aren't normally so quiet! These ones are playing games in the snow. Can you number the snowgies in the box from 1 to 5 starting with the smallest?

a ◯

b 1

c ◯

◯

d ◯

e ◯

Answer on page 68.

ALL ABOUT SVEN

Colour in this fun picture of Sven.

Sven is Kristoff's best friend, and always shows him the right thing to do. They go everywhere together and Kristoff always knows what Sven is thinking. Apart from his friends, Sven's favourite thing is a tasty carrot.

Counting Carrots

Help Sven work out how many carrots he has left to eat!
Write the number of carrots in each box, then add them up.

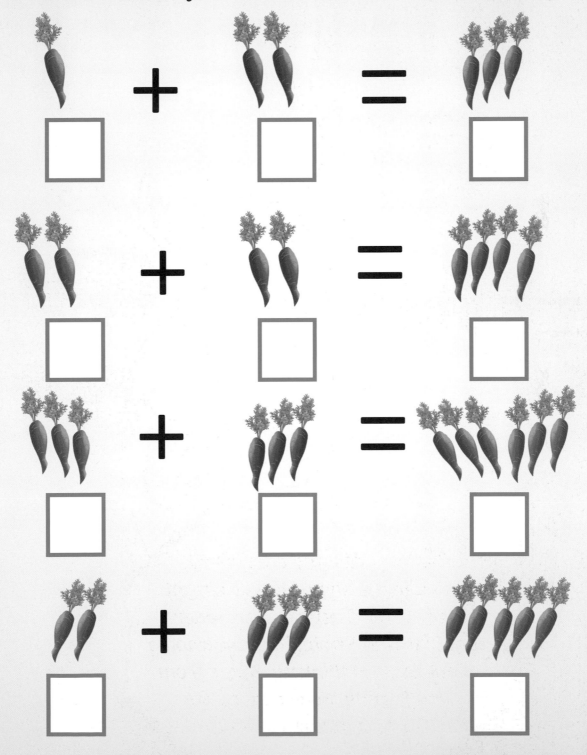

MAKE A SNOWFLAKE

Ask an adult to cut around the outside. Choose to make either (A) or (B) then follow the instructions. Photocopy the page if you want to make both shapes.

 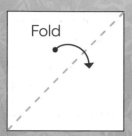

1 Fold the paper in half diagonally.

2 Fold the triangle in half.

3 Then fold one third to the front and one third to the back.

4 Trim the points off at the bottom.

5 Cut into the folds to remove the blue areas.

6 Carefully unfold your snowflake.

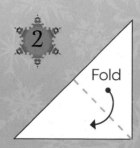

OPEN YOUR EYES

Can you spot 10 differences between these 2 scenes?
Colour in a snowflake for each one you find.

Answer on page 68.

FROSTY FUN

The blocks of ice are numbered from 1 to 9.
Can you write in the missing numbers?

1	–	3
–	5	6
–	8	–

Ice Sums

Count the number of blocks of ice that are not on the pile.

Snowy Search
Tick these items when you spot them in the scene!

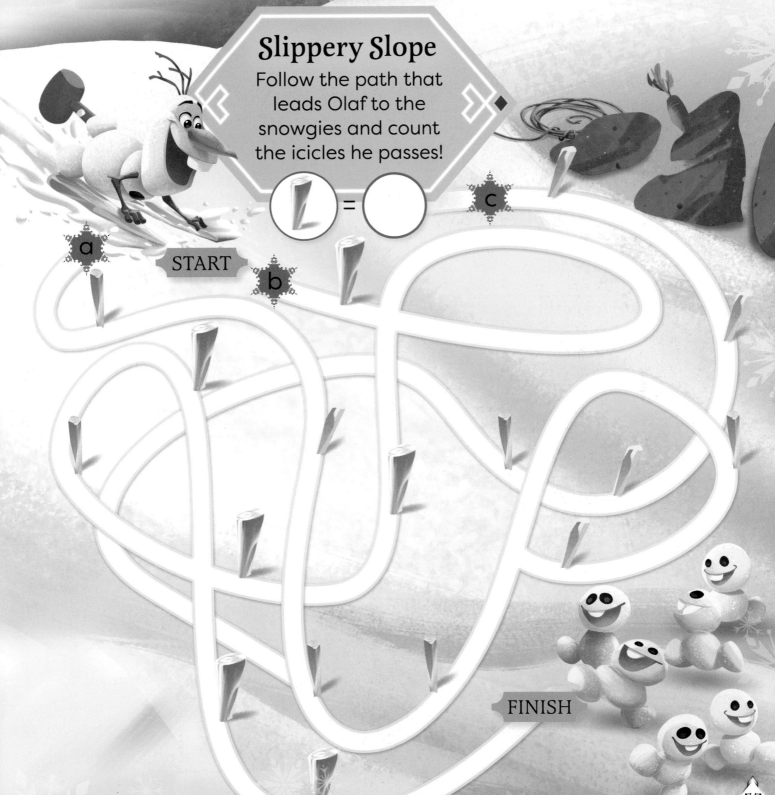

Slippery Slope
Follow the path that leads Olaf to the snowgies and count the icicles he passes!

( ) = ( )

a

b

c

START

FINISH

Answer on page 68.

ALL ABOUT THE TROLLS

Add some colour to the troll.

The trolls are magical creatures that live in the mountains. They can control the power of the Northern Lights and turn themselves into rocks! Grand Pabbie is the oldest troll and a wise healer. The trolls raised Kristoff from when he was a baby and always look out for Kristoff and his friends.

Picture Pieces

Can you work out which jigsaw piece fits into each space in the picture?

TROLL VALLEY

The trolls live in the Valley of the Living Rock, where the Northern Lights always appear. Colour in the dazzling lights in the night sky.

Troll Count

How many trolls are enjoying the Northern Lights?

Answer on page 68.

JUST ROLL WITH IT

Can you follow the word wheel round to find to Pabbie's name and three troll-related words? Write the words in the space below.

1 P _ _ _ _ _ _
2 _ O _ _ _ _ _
3 _ _ _ S _ _ _ _
4 _ _ _ I _ _ _

CREEPY SHADOWS

IT WAS A QUIET EVENING IN TROLL VALLEY, UNTIL ...

AHHH!

A MONSTEEEEEER!

HELLO! THE FIRST SHOW IS ABOUT A SNOW UNICORN ...

THE SHOW HASN'T EVEN STARTED! WHERE DID EVERYONE GO?

Manuscript: Tea Orsi; Layout: Alberto Zanon; Cleanup: Rosa La Barbera; Colour: Antonella Angrisani

The End

SHADOW SPOTTING

Olaf isn't the only one making a shadow show!
Can you match the characters to their shadows below?

Grand Pabbie

a

b

Sven

c

Kristoff

Anna

d

Answer on page 68.

READY FOR FUN?

The Trolls' party is so noisy it's hard to figure out who's saying what! Look at this scene and match the speech bubbles to the correct characters by writing their name on the line.

T _ _ _ _ _ _ _ _ TY

a
I'd like to try that pudding ...

....

Festive Banner
Complete the banner by putting the jumbled letters below in the correct spaces.
R A O L R P L

c
Let the music begin!

....

b
Ha, ha stop tickling me!

....

FROZEN FRIENDS

Find out which Frozen friend you are most like!
Read the questions and follow the arrows. If you answer YES,
follow the blue arrow. If you answer NO, follow the purple arrow.

Do you love making new friends?

NO → Do you always follow your heart?

YES → Do you you always think before you act?

NO → Are you always careful?

YES → Are you chatty?

NO → Are you always smiling?

YES

NO → Do you like cold weather?

NO → Do you always dance at parties?

YES → Is your favourite thing a warm hug?

NO

YES

NO → Are you very graceful?

NO → Do you have magical powers?

NO → Do you love summer

YES

NO

YES

NO

YES

Anna
Like Anna, you are chatty, friendly and at times a little clumsy! You love adventures and are quick to follow your heart.

Elsa
You are most like Elsa! Cool, calm and collected, you think carefully before making decisions.

Olaf
Olaf is happy, loving and cuddly ... just like you! You love summer and will do anything for your friends.

Cut along here.

Cut along here. ✂

Answers

Page 9 ELSA'S WINTER WORDS

Elsa's favourite winter words are:
ice, frozen and snow.

Page 10-11 THE KINGDOM OF ARENDELLE

1 NORTH MOUNTAIN
2 TROLL VALLEY
3 ARENDELLE
4 ICE PALACE
5 CASTLE
6 FJORD

Page 12 WINTER MAGIC

The dot-to-dot puzzle reveals
a Christmas tree.

Page 13 PALACE MEMORIES

1) Sven is standing next to Kristoff.
2) Olaf is looking at some of the snowgies.
3) Sven and Kristoff aren't made from snow.
4) No, Elsa and Anna aren't in the picture.

Page 14 A LOYAL GUARD

Picture C is the odd one out.

Page 15 HAPPY MOMENTS

Page 17 LOST IN THE SNOW

Page 20-21 A SPECIAL SNOWMAN

1. SNOW
2. C
3. 3
4. OLAF

Page 23 PUZZLING PATHS

A leads to Sven.
B leads to Kristoff.
C leads to Anna.

Page 25 FUN IN THE SUN

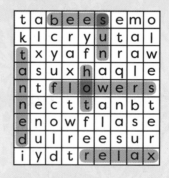

Page 28-29 Summer Trip

Page 29 LET'S GO

The friends are going to the woods.

Page 31 WARM HUGS

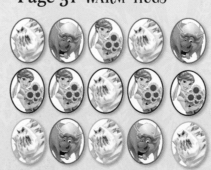

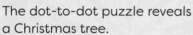

Page 39 KRISTOFF'S TITLE

Kristoff is Arendelle's Official Ice Master and Deliverer.

Page 40 SPECIAL DELIVERY

Page 41 MESSAGE

A MAGICAL BEGINNING!

Page 42 SNOW BUDDIES

1. SVEN, 2. KRISTOFF, 3. KRISTOFF,
4. SVEN, 5. KRISTOFF

Page 45 FUNNY SNOWGIES

b - 1, a - 2, c - 3, d - 4, e - 5.

Page 47 COUNTING CARROTS

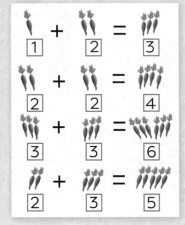

Page 51 OPEN YOUR EYES

Page 52 FROSTY FUN

Ice Sums

There are 6 blocks of ice not on the pile.

Page 53 SLIPPERY SLOPE

There are 7 icicles on route B which leads to the snowgies.

Page 55 PICTURE PIECES

1 - b, 2 - c, 3 - a, 4 - d.

Page 56 TROLL VALLEY

There are 14 trolls.

Page 57 JUST ROLL WITH IT

1 PABBIE, 2 ROCKS, 3 CRYSTAL,
4 MAGIC.

Page 59 SHADOW SPOTTING

Grand Pabbie = c
Sven = d
Kristoff = a
Anna = b

Page 60-61 READY FOR FUN?

a - Pabbie, b - Olaf, c - Kristoff,
d - Anna, e - Elsa.

Festive Banner

TROLL PARTY

GOODBYE!
Watford LRC